Dear Parent:

Your child's love of rea

Every child learns to read in a different way and at his or her own speed. Some go back and forth between reading levels and read favorite books again and again. Others read through each level in order. You can help your young reader improve and become more confident by encouraging his or her own interests and abilities. From books your child reads with you to the first books he or she reads alone, there are I Can Read Books for every stage of reading:

SHARED READING
Basic language, word repetition, and whimsical illustrations, ideal for sharing with your emergent reader

BEGINNING READING
Short sentences, familiar words, and simple concepts for children eager to read on their own

READING WITH HELP
Engaging stories, longer sentences, and language play for developing readers

READING ALONE
Complex plots, challenging vocabulary, and high-interest topics for the independent reader

I Can Read Books have introduced children to the joy of reading since 1957. Featuring award-winning authors and illustrators and a fabulous cast of beloved characters, I Can Read Books set the standard for beginning readers.

A lifetime of discovery begins with the magical words **"I Can Read!"**

Visit www.icanread.com for information on enriching your child's reading experience.

Always check with a veterinarian about how to best care for animals in your home/habitat.

To Peeka and Boo, who made it through the weekend
—O.R.-P.

To you, dear reader; enjoy reading
—L.M.

I Can Read® and I Can Read Book® are trademarks of HarperCollins Publishers.
Balzer + Bray is an imprint of HarperCollins Publishers.

Makeda Makes a Home for Subway
Text copyright © 2024 by Olugbemisola Rhuday-Perkovich
Illustrations copyright © 2024 by Lydia Mba
All rights reserved. Manufactured in Malaysia.
No part of this book may be used or reproduced in any manner whatsoever without written permission except in the case of brief quotations embodied in critical articles and reviews. For information address HarperCollins Children's Books, a division of HarperCollins Publishers, 195 Broadway, New York, NY 10007.
www.icanread.com

Library of Congress Control Number: 2023943601
ISBN 978-0-06-321728-7 (pbk) — ISBN 978-0-06-321729-4 (trade bdg)

The artist used Adobe Photoshop and Procreate to create the digital illustrations for this book.
Typography by Caitlin E. D. Stamper

24 25 26 27 28 COS 10 9 8 7 6 5 4 3 2 1

First Edition

Makeda Makes a Home for Subway

By Olugbemisola Rhuday-Perkovich
Pictures By Lydia Mba

BALZER + BRAY
An Imprint of HarperCollinsPublishers

Makeda made marvelous things.

Like tiny fancy cakes for tea

and models of faraway galaxies.

Sometimes she made sparkly slime

and even noise at quiet time.

Subway, the class guinea pig,

did not make noise at quiet time.

Subway was quiet almost all of the time.

He was not like MC,

the guinea pig in another class.

MC squeaked in her cage.

She whooshed through her tunnel

and swooped down her slide.

Subway did not whoosh or swoop.

His cage did not have rides.

He only had a paper ball to push.

“Subway’s cage is no fun,”

said Makeda.

“We are looking at the Word Wall now, not Subway,” said Ms. Evelyn.
Who can tell us what S-A-D spells?”
“Maybe Subway is S-A-D
in his boring cage,” said Makeda.
“We should get a class puppy,” said Lu.
Ms. Evelyn sighed.
“It seems that
Word Wall time is over.”

I will make Subway
a marvelous cage, thought Makeda.
Then he will not be S-A-D.

Class guinea pigs went home
with a different kid every weekend.
"I can take Subway home this time,"
Makeda said.

Makeda had not asked her family
about bringing Subway home.
So they had not said “No.”

Makeda's grandpa, Daddy Squared,
picked her up from school.
"Thank you for hosting Subway,"
Ms. Evelyn said to him.
"This is a surprise,"
said Daddy Squared.

The rest of her family
was also surprised.
“Keep him on your side of the room,”
Makeda’s sister, Candace, said.

“Subway needs to have more fun,”
said Makeda.
“I will make rides for his cage
like they have at FunPlay Land.
He can whoosh and swoop like MC.”

The rest of her family

was also surprised.

“Keep him on your side of the room,”

Makeda’s sister, Candace, said.

"Subway needs to have more fun,"
said Makeda.
"I will make rides for his cage
like they have at FunPlay Land.
He can whoosh and swoop like MC."

“FunPlay Land is not for pets,”
said Daddy. “It is for kids.”
“We should all go to FunPlay Land!”
said Makeda’s brother, James.

Makeda's best friend, Glory,

came over to help.

"MC has a tunnel and a slide,"

said Makeda.

"Let's make a deluxe tunnel-slide

for Subway.

That will be really fun."

"I am scared of tunnels," said Glory.

"Maybe Subway is too."

"Not me," said Makeda.

They made a big fancy tunnel-slide.

But Subway did not whoosh or swoop.

He just turned away.

Makeda and Glory sat and thought.

"I like when my legs go back and forth

on the swing at FunPlay Land,"

said Makeda.

"Let's make Subway a swing!"

Glory looked at Subway.

"He has short legs," she said.

"Maybe he can't swing them."

"Subway has four legs," said Makeda.

"So maybe he will like swinging even more."

But Subway did not like the swing.

He just kept pushing his paper ball.

Makeda and Glory thought some more.

"Let's make something *super* fun,"

said Makeda.

"Like the FunPlay Land Monster Coaster!"

"I like the Lazy River Float better,"

said Glory.

"Not me," said Makeda.

They made a roller coaster
with a shoebox and toy train tracks.
They rolled Subway up and down.
“Whee!” said Makeda.
Subway hissed and hid behind his ball.

Momma came into the room.

"I made Subway a treat," she said.

"Bananas, apples, and blueberries.

But why does everyone look sad?"

"We made a fun cage like MC's,

but Subway will not play like MC,"

said Makeda.

Momma put the treat in the cage.

Subway made *chut chut* sounds.

He ate his treat. He purred.

"He is happy now," said Momma.

"*MC* likes kiwi and plums," said Glory.

“I understand!” said Makeda.

We both like FunPlay Land,

but we don’t like all the same rides.

Subway is not MC.

And he is not S-A-D.

He was already happy in his own way.”

"Let's find out what else
Subway likes," said Glory.

They read Ms. Evelyn's

Subway Care Sheet.

It said he liked a clean cage,

paper balls, and fruit salad.

The girls cleaned Subway's cage.

They played music and danced
while they cleaned.
Subway twirled!
“Subway likes music!” said Makeda.

Subway pushed his paper ball!

"Yay!" cheered the girls.

"He looks very happy," said Makeda.

“I am happy and hungry,” said Glory.

The friends made a mango salad.

It was a marvelous snack.

"What will we do
with the tunnel-slide and swing?"
asked Glory.
"I have an idea!" said Makeda.
They made toy guinea pigs
from yarn and felt.
The toy guinea pigs whooshed
and swooped on the rides.

“These guinea pigs are not
like Subway or MC,” said Makeda.
But all of them are marvelous!”